This book
belongs to:

_____

_____

This edition first published in Great Britain by HarperCollins Publishers Ltd in 2000

1 3 5 7 9 10 8 6 4 2

ISBN: 0 00 710787 0

A CIP catalogue for this title is available from the British Library.

Reproduction by Graphic Studio S.rl. Verona
Printed in Italy by Garzanti Verga S.rl.

NODDY IN TOYLAND

Mr Straw's New Cow

Collins

An imprint of HarperCollinsPublishers

It was a very busy morning on Mr Straw's farm. All the animals had to be fed, the cows had to be milked and the eggs had to be collected. Mrs Straw usually fed the animals, but she wasn't there today. She had gone to look after her sister who was ill.

PARP! PARP!
Noddy drove into the farmyard.

"Hello, Noddy my lad, what can I do for you?" asked Mr Straw, rushing out to meet the car.

"Mrs Straw asked me yesterday if I would lend you a hand," explained Noddy. "But I've got TWO hands you can borrow if you want!"

"Well, I could do with some help, Noddy my lad," agreed Mr Straw. "Can you feed the hens?"

"Yes I can," said Noddy.

When Noddy picked up the sack of corn, the hens clucked and scratched around his feet.

"Here you are, hens! Breakfast!" laughed Noddy,
as he scattered the corn on the ground.
His bell JINGLED merrily as
he worked.

MOO!

"That's a funny hen!" cried Noddy. He turned
round. A cow was standing behind him, and she
was looking at Noddy with enormous eyes.

"Shoo!" shouted Noddy.

"It's all right, Noddy. That's my new cow," said
Mr Straw who was walking across the farmyard.

"She only wants to be friends. Could you collect
the eggs now, please?"

Noddy fetched the basket and placed the eggs into it very carefully. He had just picked up the last one, when there was a loud MOO!

Noddy was so startled that he dropped the egg.

SPLAT!

Mr Straw's new cow was right behind Noddy,
breathing down his neck.

"You naughty cow," grumbled Noddy. "You frightened me. Shoo! GO AWAY!"

"It looks like she's your best friend now, Noddy my lad!" laughed Mr Straw. "I can manage the rest of the feeding, but could you take six eggs to Mrs Tubby Bear for me?"

Mr Straw gave Noddy the eggs and three sixpences for all his help.

"Thank you, Noddy," said Mr Straw. "Don't forget to close the gate as you leave."

Noddy drove out of the farmyard. Then as he was closing the gate, Mr Straw's new cow began to run towards him.

"Shoo! Go away!" shouted Noddy. He leapt
into his car and drove away as fast as he
could. Noddy was in such a hurry that he
forgot to close the gate. Mr Straw's new cow
ran out of the farmyard after his friend.

On the farm it was almost milking time.

"Now, where's that new cow of mine?"
Mr Straw asked himself. He looked around
the farmyard and saw the open gate.

"I told Noddy to close the gate," grumbled the
farmer. "Now my new cow has followed him. Come
on, horse. We'll have to find her."

Mr Straw climbed on to his horse and rode out
of the farmyard.

He made sure that the gate was closed this time,
so that all the other animals would be safe.

"I think we'll try Mrs Tubby Bear's house first,"
Mr Straw said.

"NEIGH!" the horse agreed.

What a sight greeted Mr Straw, as he rode up to
Mrs Tubby Bear's house! On her washing line was a
pair of Mr Tubby Bear's trousers with their legs
badly chewed.

A muddy pillowcase lay on the grass and a sheet covered in hoof marks was wrapped around a tree.

"This is your cow's fault, Mr Straw," said Mrs Tubby Bear angrily.

"I am sorry," apologised the farmer. "Is the cow still here?"

"Indeed it is not!" replied Mrs Tubby Bear. "Noddy brought in my eggs and, when he left, the cow followed him."

"And where did Noddy go?" asked Mr Straw anxiously.

"He went to see Tessie Bear," replied Mrs Tubby Bear.

"I must go there at once,"
shouted Mr Straw, and he
galloped off through
Toy Town.

As Mr Straw's horse CLIP-CLOPPED up to
Tessie Bear's house, out rushed Bumpy Dog.

WOOF!

WOOF!

"Bumpy Dog is very excited," sighed Tessie Bear.

"One of your cows frightened him in the garden. Then the cow ate all my flowers."

"I am sorry," said Mr Straw. "Is the cow still here?"

"No," replied Tessie Bear. "I think she was waiting for Noddy, because when he left, the cow followed after him."

"And where was Noddy going?" asked Mr Straw anxiously.

"He went to see Big-Ears," replied Tessie Bear.

"Then I must go there too!" shouted Mr Straw, and he galloped off towards Toadstool House.

PARP! PARP!

Noddy's car
was outside
Big-Ears' house.
So was Mr Straw's
new cow. She was trying
to eat Noddy's steering wheel.
When Big-Ears and Noddy heard the CLIP-CLOP
of Mr Straw's horse, they came rushing outside.

"Go away, cow!" shouted Noddy. "Why are YOU here?"

"She followed you through the open gate," explained Mr Straw. "But I wonder, why is she so fond of you, Noddy?"

Noddy scratched his chin and shook his head.

JINGLE

As soon as the cow heard Noddy's bell, she bounded towards him and tried to pull the hat from Noddy's head.

"It's your BELL she likes!" laughed Mr Straw.

"I will buy her one of her own," said Noddy. "Then she won't need to follow me any more!"

"MOO!" said the cow, with pleasure.

THE END

Here are some more books for you to enjoy:

Noddy's Bumper Activity Book
ISBN: 0-00-710640-8

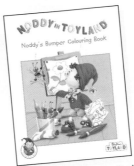

Noddy's Bumper Colouring Book
ISBN: 0-00-710639-4

The Goblins and the Ice Cream
ISBN: 0-00-710786-2

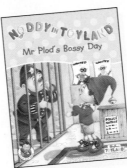

Mr Plod's Bossy Day
ISBN: 0-00-710789-7

Bumpy Dog Helps Out
ISBN: 0-00-710788-9

Noddy's and the Runaway Cakes
ISBN: 0-00-710637-8

Noddy's Special Whistle
ISBN: 0-00-710638-6